Emilie's Voltaire

by Arthur Giron

A SAMUEL FRENCH ACTING EDITION

SAMUEL FRENCH

FOUNDED 1830

NEW YORK HOLLYWOOD LONDON TORONTO

SAMUELFRENCH.COM

MUSIC USE NOTE

Licensees are solely responsible for obtaining formal written permission from copyright owners to use copyrighted music in the performance of this play and are strongly cautioned to do so. If no such permission is obtained by the licensee, then the licensee must use only original music that the licensee owns and controls. Licensees are solely responsible and liable for all music clearances and shall indemnify the copyright owners of the play and their licensing agent, Samuel French, Inc., against any costs, expenses, losses and liabilities arising from the use of music by licensees.

IMPORTANT BILLING AND CREDIT REQUIREMENTS

All producers of *EMILIE'S VOLTAIRE: A LOVE STORY must* give credit to the Author of the Play in all programs distributed in connection with performances of the Play, and in all instances in which the title of the Play appears for the purposes of advertising, publicizing or otherwise exploiting the Play and/or a production. The name of the Author *must* appear on a separate line on which no other name appears, immediately following the title and *must* appear in size of type not less than fifty percent of the size of the title type.

EMILIE'S VOLTAIRE was first produced by the Living Image Arts Theatre Company in New York City on January 15, 2009. The performance was directed by Kevin Confoy, with sets by Jito Lee, costumes by Carol Pelletier, lighting by Jake DeGroot, and sound design by Geoffrey Roecker. The cast was as follows:

EMILIE . . . . .Amy Lynn Stewart

VOLTAIRE. . . . . .Michael Medeiros

EMILIE'S VOLTAIRE was the winner of the Galileo Prize.

CHARACTERS

Emilie
Voltaire

SETTING

Paris

TIME

New Year's Eve, 1733

To Mariluz, the love of my life.
A.G.

ACT ONE

(The bells of Notre Dame ring eleven, New Year's Eve. Paris, 1733. On the Left Bank of the Seine lives **VOLTAIRE***. On fire, at the peak of his powers, he is writing in his bath, his scratched and bloody knees poking up. Near-to-hand is a large cup of coffee and a telescope. A kettle of additional bath water is heating on a tall, beautiful porcelain stove. Candles burn, cushions at his back. He writes with furious intensity. A blood-stained bandage is wrapped around a head wound.)*

VOLTAIRE. Can a man of humble birth hope for love from a high-born beauty? It was New Year's Eve in Paris the night she changed his miserable life. Our stupid, though handsome, hero was invited to see the royal fireworks from the terrace of a treacherous aristocrat. He was standing behind a beautiful woman seated at a gaming table when a footman whispered to him that he was wanted outside on an urgent matter. Once he stepped out the front door, he only had time to see the coat of arms on the carriage of that eunuch the Chevalier de Ass-hole and to hear the coward cry, "Now you will be taught a real lesson, philosopher!" whereupon he tossed his latest book into the mud and ordered a gang of cutthroats to knock out my brains.

(He grabs his head, moans.)

Oh, my poor head! No! The anti-intellectual forces are not going to kill me. They're not going to kill me! This is war!

(He goes back to writing.)

VOLTAIRE. *(cont.)* Beaten black and blue and left for dead, our hero dragged himself back into the party where his aristocratic friends, instead of being sympathetic, laughed at him.

(stops writing, hears laughter, jeers.)

STOP YOUR LAUGHING! I AM A MAN! I DEMAND SATISFACTION!

(A woman cackles. He continues to write.)

The Queen, that Polish witch, joined in the gales of derisive laughter. And the lesson he learned was that no amount of work, no amount of achievement, would ever keep this unloved commoner from being an outcast. When suddenly –

EMILIE. *(off)* Monsieur Voltaire! The upstart poet Voltaire! Blasphemer, worshipper of Venus, corrupter of morals, playwright –

VOLTAIRE. Who has entered through my secret door? I must employ my system of reflecting mirrors.

(He points his telescope at a mirror hanging at the entrance, angled to reflect another framed mirror in the hallway. The image seen is of a woman searching. She carries a candle. He makes sounds of approval.)

Is she a courtesan? How did she get my private key?

EMILIE. *(off)* Answer when your better calls! Where are you? I smell the aroma of coffee….

(He hides his telescope.)

Coffee, coffee!

VOLTAIRE. Stay out! I'm working!

*(**EMILIE** enters dramatically. She holds high a tall candle. A statuesque beauty, she wears extraordinary diamonds under a flowing fur-lined, snow-flecked cape and hood. A golden half-mask covers her eyes, and brilliant star-shaped clips hold up mountains of luminous hair. Beat.)*

EMILIE. Gentlemen rise when I enter a room.

VOLTAIRE. *(aside)* I want to bite her.

Who gave you the coveted key to my secret door?

EMILIE. A friend at court.

VOLTAIRE. Bring your tongue closer.

EMILIE. I cannot.

VOLTAIRE. Why not? Pray tell?

EMILIE. Because I am not here.

VOLTAIRE. Oh, I'm sorry you did not come. I would have offered you a forbidden cup of coffee.

EMILIE. *(aside)* Coffee!

VOLTAIRE. It is unfortunate the mayor decreed that caffeine makes women too excitable.

EMILIE. *(aside)* I have a passion for coffee.

VOLTAIRE. I have devised a way to protect a woman's reputation. There is a trap door, a lift that rises from the kitchen. It contains a second cup and a pot of coffee.

(She lifts a trap door where there is a cup and a coffee pot.)

Rules are for other people. Let us break the decree against women drinking coffee. Conversation and coffee go hand-in-hand.

*(She drinks, moans in pleasure. She drinks again at the same time that **VOLTAIRE** drinks again. Both moan together.)*

BOTH. Mmmmm. Ahhhh…

VOLTAIRE. I've sweetened it with almond liqueur and a favorite spice –

EMILIE. Cinnamon.

(They finish the last drops in their cups and react as above.)

BOTH. Mnnn. Ahhhh.

EMILIE. Sinful.

VOLTAIRE. Ah, a Protestant.

EMILIE. No. A daughter of Rome.

VOLTAIRE. Rome has always decided in favor of the opinion which most degrades the human mind.

EMILIE. There is only one morality as there is only one geometry.

VOLTAIRE. Why haven't I met you? Did you appear in society while I was in England? *(aside)* Never have I spoken of morality and geometry so close to midnight.

(She places the dirty cups in the trap door.)

Your perfume is beguiling…familiar…There are exciting changes in the air.

EMILIE. Treasonous changes.

VOLTAIRE. Undress. Join me. I do not believe in the separation of the sexes. Although women are less complete than men.

EMILIE. Dare one ask why?

VOLTAIRE. Because women have fewer teeth. At least that's what the great Aristotle believed. And no one has contradicted him for over 2,000 years. Let us investigate his findings tonight.

EMILIE. You question Aristotle?!

VOLTAIRE. I am the doubter and the doubt. Undress. We will count your teeth and make history tonight. My bath accommodates two. You come here uninvited. And, yet, you present yourself in a haughty, conventional fashion with your face covered…?

EMILIE. We are separated by class, Monsieur. One must respect the world as it is – whatever is, is right.

VOLTAIRE. Blow out the candle. I make love in the dark.

EMILIE. *(aside)* I must seduce him. But on my terms not his. I need money.

VOLTAIRE. You are burning up good money. I spend on expensive tapers that don't smoke since I write day and night one hundred letters a day; pamphlets, poems, plays. I expose myself totally when I put pen to paper.

EMILIE. You've given me so many hours of pleasure on the page. I could never be introduced to you, of course, but, I decided to take matters into my own hands…I need to express my disapproval of such cowardice. To set cutthroats on you to club out your brains. They tried to unman you. Oh, if we lived in a meritocracy, you would be the most manly man of all.

VOLTAIRE. *(quietly)* You were there tonight?

EMILIE. Sir, these are dangerous times, you must learn to be less truthful. Or you will suffer at the hands of mediocre minds.

VOLTAIRE. The world as it is, is not right. I will never cease to attack tyranny and persecution by a privileged orthodoxy in Church and State.

EMILIE. The fruit of your incendiary thoughts blossom all over your flesh, the scratches on your knees, the cuts on your elbows make traceries on your brave body like fine brocade.

VOLTAIRE. *(aside)* I love women and words.

EMILIE. Let me warm your water.

VOLTAIRE. My water is boiling.

EMILIE. Nonsense.

(She picks up the kettle and approaches the tub.)

VOLTAIRE. Don't look at my body.

(Nevertheless, he spreads his legs and she pours hot water between them. He moans with pleasure.)

Oh, mmm, ahhh!

EMILIE. Oh! Am I burning you?

VOLTAIRE. Keep pouring.

(Almost unconsciously, calmly, she begins to unwind his bloody bandage. Through the following, she functions like a nurse, tending his head wound.)

I was thinking here bleeding, that I may never find an equal. Before you came in, I was praying for God to grant me a companion. He is a selfish, ungiving father to me. He has never permitted me to know fulfillment.

EMILIE. You have never experienced ecstasy?

VOLTAIRE. *(shrugs)* Pleasure.

EMILIE. Pleasure is not enough.

VOLTAIRE. Pleasure is Hell.

EMILIE. Well, said.

   (aside)

   He inspires naked honesty in me.

   There is always a war in me between reason and passion.

VOLTAIRE. Reason! Reason!

EMILIE. Ah, pen and paper….are you working on a new play?

   (She boldly approaches his bath.)

VOLTAIRE. Get your finger out of my ink pot!

EMILIE. I was curious to know how you achieve such potency on the page. Mmmm. This isn't ink. In what do you dip your pen?

VOLTAIRE. Blood and bile.

EMILIE. Then you transform your grievances into gold.

VOLTAIRE. My feelings are my fortune, yes.

EMILIE. You invest the page.

VOLTAIRE. I am prepared to die for my beliefs.

EMILIE. You almost did tonight.

VOLTAIRE. I refuse to die until I've been elected to the Academy and join the ranks of the immortals.

EMILIE. You forever put forward your candidacy when a seat becomes vacant. Time after time, your candidacy is rejected. You were beaten black and blue tonight because you persist in provoking everyone! How else should patriotic Frenchmen respond to you when your "Philosophical Letters From England" are so critical of us? The book is sold everywhere! You make a fortune at our expense, my expense.

VOLTAIRE. What good does it do me to have wealth, if I have no one to share it with?

EMILIE. You need a woman who can spend your money.

VOLTAIRE. Preferably an extravagant woman.

EMILIE. You have THAT much money?

VOLTAIRE. My friend the Turkish Ambassador introduced me to coffee. I decided to import it. Coffee is now selling for 80 francs a pound. My coffee earnings purchase furs from North America and now all of Paris is wrapped in them. And, of course, the brainless aristocrats who despise me, borrow from me at 33 percent and make me rich.

EMILIE. But how did your fortune start, since you descend from no one?

VOLTAIRE. I descend from Homer. I come from a great line of story-tellers.

EMILIE. I descend from Euclid. Who taught me that numbers do not lie.

VOLTAIRE. I keep printing presses humming with my poems, histories, essays, stories. My publishers grow richer every day. I am read throughout Europe. My 60 plays fill the world's theaters. I write roles for intelligent women in the hope that someday I might find a gifted artist who might embody the woman of my dreams.

EMILIE. To perform in one of your masterworks…what joy! Monsieur, in all humility I say that I would be content to play the smallest part – But I would require one minor condition.

VOLTAIRE. What condition?

EMILIE. That no matter what the role, I be allowed to wear my collection of diamonds.

(She turns her back to the audience and opens her cape, then sinks into a low curtsy. He gasps at the vision of her low-cut bodice.)

VOLTAIRE. I recognize you now.

EMILIE. Because of my famous diamonds.

VOLTAIRE. Because of your famous breasts, Madame, made rosy by rouge. All the ladies now follow your fashion. Tonight, I saw your pink cherubic globes when I

VOLTAIRE. *(cont.)* looked down over your shoulders as you intently were playing at cards. The men you challenged across the table couldn't keep their eyes off the sight of your nipples. And they paid you a fortune for the privilege of losing. You took no notice of me whatsoever. Although I do not rise, please know that my body is saluting you.

EMILIE. Do not belittle me, Monsieur. I won at cards not because of my nipples, but because I was applying probability calculations.

VOLTAIRE. Ah, yes, your husband the great general has suffered ridicule because you are closeted for hours with your mathematics teacher.

EMILIE. Judge me for my own merits, or lack of them, but do not look upon me as a mere appendage to this great general or that renowned scholar. I am in my own right a whole person, responsible to myself alone for all that I am, all that I say, all that I do. It may be that there are metaphysicians and philosophers whose learning is greater than mine, although I have not met them. When I add the sum total of my graces, I confess that I am inferior to no one. I gamble to make money to buy books.

VOLTAIRE. Gabrielle Emilie, Marquise du Chatelet.

(He removes her gold mask.)

I can't believe my fortune…Venus….

EMILIE. Don't look at me. I am too large, too clumsy.

VOLTAIRE. Your colossal limbs disturb me. I am at your mercy lying here in my bath. My brain has gone. Clearly, you turn all men into pigs.

EMILIE. I am not Circe.

VOLTAIRE. You've read our classical forefathers?

EMILIE. I've always believed it could be important for a man and woman to share the same literary references.

VOLTAIRE. So then you share books with a man at bedtime.

EMILIE. *(She laughs.)* In France, men do not go to bed to read. I am laughed at, Monsieur, because I carry books wherever I go. People laugh at me the way you were laughed at tonight. I am an embarrassment to my family.

VOLTAIRE. So, you wander through the world alone, as I do.

EMILIE. Who is there in the world who can affirm my existence…? Early, I learned the sorrow of disappointing my parents by not being a conventional daughter. My energy was such that I rode horses. I wrestled trees. Naturally, I tore my gowns and my stockings. My young knees were always as bloody as yours are tonight. Soon, it was clear to my horrified mother that I was a freak of nature and would never marry. So, secretly, my father engaged tutors to educate me in Greek and Latin. I fell in love with mathematics and natural philosophy. And, quietly, the best scientists began arriving at my parlor to amuse me. The new science became my calling. I begged to attend the Wednesday meetings of scientists in the King's library at the Louvre. Never! Females are not permitted to attend! And I was forbidden, of course, ever to speak of my love for reading.

(He takes her hand.)

VOLTAIRE. Children suffer. What happened then?

EMILIE. To everyone's surprise, myself included, I began to transform. I developed a healthy body.

VOLTAIRE. To appear on stage only wearing diamonds… What a startling idea. I don't think an unclothed actress has ever appeared on the stage. The cavaliers in the town would fall all over themselves to purchase seats on the stage.

EMILIE. Monsieur Voltaire, you misunderstand. I do not perform in Paris.

VOLTAIRE. Where do you perform?

EMILIE. In my husband's estate in the country. Florent uses the forest to go hunting, so he doesn't give a fig that the medieval buildings are in such a frightful condition. In the daytime, I read, write and attempt scientific experiments. And, when the sun has set, I perform with my neighborhood friends – the Duke de Richelieu, the King of Poland...

VOLTAIRE. Stanislaus, the father of the Queen, ugh.

EMILIE. Don't make fun. It is because of the Queen that I am here, Monsieur.

VOLTAIRE. Oh?

EMILIE. Alas! I owe her a great sum of money. After I defeated the men tonight, Maria Leszcynska sat at my table, challenged me. I couldn't refuse. And I lost of course. She has given the order that I am not permitted to leave Paris tonight unless I cancel my debt to her. All the gates are closed to my carriage. And I must away to the country at once. I am informed that you loan money to members of the court.

VOLTAIRE. The Queen cheats at cards.

(Horrified, she makes sure no one has heard him.)

EMILIE. Quiet! Or we will both be locked up in the Bastille. You should never have whispered that to me while I was playing!

VOLTAIRE. You heard me then?

EMILIE. The Queen heard.

VOLTAIRE. You could have paid the witch with your diamonds.

EMILIE. Ever since paper money was introduced, it is the rage, the fashion. My debt cannot be canceled in gold, silver, or diamonds. She demands crisp stacks of beautiful, new bank notes like the ones her rival Madame de Pompadour carries tucked into a sweet purse that hangs on a chain from her waist. Pompadour gave me the key to your secret door. She says you keep great quantitieses of money about to bribe the secret police who are forever searching your house for subversive manuscripts. After you were beaten tonight the Chevalier's kinsmen conspired to have you thrown into the Bastille. I heard them say they wanted the soldiers to put hot pokers in your eyes – blind you. So, I rushed ahead to get the money before it was too late. And to warn you, of course, to escape. My coachman will alert us at the first sign of musketeers. Everyone in Paris, is paralyzed, waiting to see the fireworks, soldiers included. They're all carousing, celebrating the New Year. But we don't have much time.

VOLTAIRE. I will give you the cash, if you give me a place in your carriage.

(He begins to dry himself.)

EMILIE. That is out of the question!

VOLTAIRE. Why do you want to flee the city so quickly?

EMILIE. If you can divine my purpose tonight, I will give you refuge in my carriage. And if you can't, not only will you give me the money I need – not as a loan, but as an outright gift – you will give me…a generous supply of these expensive candles that do not smoke. And, perhaps, a pound of coffee.

VOLTAIRE. And if I win, I will demand satisfaction.

EMILIE. Agreed.

Why do I desperately want to get to the countryside?

VOLTAIRE. To spend the New Year with your children.

EMILIE. No, my son Louis is learning soldiering from his father in Prussia. I had another son, Victor, who died in childbirth, I almost died as well. Why do I want to avoid the display of fireworks?

VOLTAIRE. In the country I look up and see the stars more clearly.

(He jumps up, wrapping a large fur towel around himself.)

Tonight there is going to be a meteor shower!

EMILIE. Just so. And I want to see it.

VOLTAIRE. As do I. Have you studied the heavens through a reflecting telescope?

EMILIE. No.

VOLTAIRE. I have one. I obtained it in London.

EMILIE. Oh! Show it to me!

(He begins to dress.)

VOLTAIRE. I have a counter proposal. Since the Queen has sent word to the gatekeepers to stop your carriage, let us take mine. Unlike yours, my carriage has no coat of arms. I met my coachman Maurice in prison. He is ready 24 hours a day to help me flee. I will have a late dinner packed for us in a basket. I will take my telescope. And we will keep the money you owe the Queen for ourselves!

EMILIE. You are a scoundrel.

VOLTAIRE. Do you agree?

(banging on the door)

EMILIE. That is *my* coachman warning that musketeers are approaching.

VOLTAIRE. We can escape through the secret door.

(banging)

EMILIE. It would be a scandal.

VOLTAIRE. Break the rules.

(banging)

EMILIE. If we're caught – the Bastille.

VOLTAIRE. I wrote my first play in the Bastille.

(banging)

EMILIE. I've never been so afraid!

VOLTAIRE. I live in fear – but I live!

(more forceful banging)

EMILIE. We will be banished. Never permitted to return to Paris.

VOLTAIRE. The meteor shower awaits.

EMILIE. And the milky way.

VOLTAIRE. And the milky way.

VOLTAIRE. Permit me to affirm your existence. You have a mind. Come, step into my carriage.

(He extends his hand and after a second she takes it and steps into his tub, which becomes a coach. Lanterns appear up front. Bright moonlight. Swirling snow.)

Maurice –

*(to **EMILIE**)*

Which road?

EMILIE. Toward Paradise.

VOLTAIRE. Lorraine.

EMILIE. Lorraine.

VOLTAIRE. I love Lorraine. Whereabouts?

EMILIE. A little corner of Champagne.

VOLTAIRE. MAURICE, NORTH TO CHAMPAGNE! Stop at nothing! We are being pursued! Fly before the horses are frightened by the blasted fireworks. Go! Or it is a cold dungeon for us! Go!

(The crack of a whip. Sounds of horses, wheels crunching on mud and ice. He wraps furs around her.)

The stars await you.

EMILIE. Why do you love Lorraine?

VOLTAIRE. Because it is the road to freedom. Close to the border with Flanders and, then, the world. Freedom!

EMILIE. Freedom

EMILIE. Did you bring the money?

VOLTAIRE. Enough to escape to Great Britain, should we need to.

EMILIE. But you are giving me the Queen's portion, are you not?

VOLTAIRE. The agreement was that if I guessed the reason you wanted to leave town, I didn't have to give you anything.

EMILIE. Stop the coach.

VOLTAIRE. You are not a gentleman.

EMILIE. Whenever I allow emotions to cloud my reason, it goes badly for me. Stop the coach! I command it.

VOLTAIRE. You cannot command my coachman.

EMILIE. So I am being abducted?

VOLTAIRE. Yes.

EMILIE. STOP!

VOLTAIRE. Maurice has been trained not to be alarmed unduly by the surprising behavior of young Parisians. Do you think that ideas arise from emotion? Or does emotion rise out of ideas?

EMILIE. Hush. I am thinking of hurling myself out this door.

VOLTAIRE. Leave your diamonds behind. Your body will be covered in mud and blood.

EMILIE. I have been jumping from various heights all my life and always land on my feet. Making leaps is my specialty. Experimentation is in my nature.

VOLTAIRE. *(aside)* She is both conventional AND experimental. What a tortured person. I must save her.

If you jump and survive, wild boars will devour you, we are riding near the king's hunting preserve. Yes, this area has been cultivated to breed fierce boars with sharp tusks. I see tusks shinning out there in the moonlight. Flaming, beady eyes.

Listen! Horses!

(sound of horses)

EMILIE. We are being pursued! The Queen has sent her guards after us.

VOLTAIRE. Or the Furies.

EMILIE. The Furies! Yes!

VOLTAIRE. It *is* important to share the same literary references.

Maurice! Faster! Faster!

EMILIE. Oh, I am going to die tonight. I always knew I would die young.

VOLTAIRE. I brought my pistol. I will protect you.

(She laughs.)

EMILIE. You put me in danger.

(The carriage sways.)

VOLTAIRE. The road is covered with a sheet of ice. And these treacherous curves –

EMILIE. Chaos! Think. Philosopher think. Let us unharness the horses and ride on ahead.

VOLTAIRE. And leave the basket of food and wine?

(In the distance, the sounds of exploding fireworks. Sound of the horses reacting in fright.)

EMILIE. The fireworks! From the palace!

(The carriage tips over. He grabs **EMILIE.** *Chaos. Sounds of the crash, horses, screams. Then, silence and bright moonlight. A dog barks in the distance. A carriage wheel spins.)*

VOLTAIRE. Open your eyes Gabrielle Emilie, Marquise du Chatelet.

(He kisses her.)

Awaken.

EMILIE. Am I dead?

VOLTAIRE. All your prejudices have died. We must clear out. So the carriage can be righted.

(He climbs out.)

Maurice, my good fellow, have the men help you stand the carriage upright. Tell them I will pay them handsomely to tell the Queen that we escaped into the night Here is a bag of gold for them to celebrate the New Year. Emilie, come. Let's have a midnight picnic. You see the top of the hill white with virgin snow? We will spread out fur rugs and pillows. We'll wait up there. Maurice, blow your trumpet when it is safe to continue. Oh, how beautiful.

What happened to our meteor shower?

EMILIE. I saw stars when we tipped over.

VOLTAIRE. Me, too. You banged your head against my testicles. There is nothing more painful.

EMILIE. Men are such babies about their bodies.

VOLTAIRE. How do you know?

EMILIE. I spend time at the veterans hospital, caring and feeding the wounded, the abandoned, the dying. I love men when they're sick. I much prefer unhealthy men than healthy men.

God save me from huge, heroic males! Hunters. Who prefer the out-of-doors. No. Give me a man on his back, whom I can read to. The more they suffer, the more my heart enlarges, spiritually, emotionally....

VOLTAIRE. Really?

EMILIE. When I saw you, I wanted to change your diaper, I mean your bandage. You looked, not like a man in his bath, but like a baby in his crib.

VOLTAIRE. Then you have maternal feelings? May I tell you about my birth?

EMILIE. Of course.

VOLTAIRE. I almost died.

EMILIE. No!

VOLTAIRE. Yes! I was so close to death, I was baptized at home.

EMILIE. That serious?

VOLTAIRE. All those who surrounded my cradle assumed that my stay on this corrupt earth would be a brief one. Death always stands at my elbow. No one knows this...but you.

EMILIE. You suffer...still?

VOLTAIRE. If I can experience two hours without pain, I am content.

EMILIE. No.

VOLTAIRE. Yes.

(She quickly and efficiently, spreads out the rugs, cushions and opens the basket, takes out a brocade tablecloth, fine silver that shines, crystal for wine, plates.)

EMILIE. Please, tell me. What are your complaints?

(Through the following, he opens a bottle of wine and fills two glasses.)

VOLTAIRE. Catarrh, dysentery, itch, smallpox, the grippe, fever, chronic colic, erysipelas, gout, apoplexy, inflammation of the lungs, scurvy, rheumatism, strangury, deafness, indigestion, dropsy, falling hair, loss of voice, neuritis, blindness, and paralysis. I have but a moment to live.

EMILIE. No.

VOLTAIRE. Yes.

(He toasts.)

To your health in the New Year.

EMILIE. To *yours.*

(They drink.)

VOLTAIRE. May I drink another toast – to my mother.

EMILIE. Oh, yes.

(They drink.)

She died young?

(He nods.)

Then, how did you learn about women?

VOLTAIRE. I know nothing about women.

EMILIE. You have never been in love?

(He shakes his head. While he drinks, she begins eating with gusto. Slowly, through the following, the dawn begins to appear.)

VOLTAIRE. But I remember being held by my mother. Tightly. Her body racked by storms of coughing.

EMILIE. She died of consumption, then?

VOLTAIRE. When I was seven.

EMILIE. I have observed that the fires of genius burn in the children of consumptive mothers – if they live.

VOLTAIRE. Why did I live?

EMILIE. To become a…a trumpet for your times.
What were you called when you were little?

VOLTAIRE. You'll never know, Madame. I hate to tell you, but have you noticed that we are out-of-doors?

EMILIE. This is the most beautiful room in all of France.

VOLTAIRE. The key to the entire universe lies before you.

EMILIE. What do you see that I don't.

VOLTAIRE. The attraction of bodies – celestial, earthly. It is one of the Laws of the great Newton. Our carriage fell, an apple falls. He discovered gravity, the natural pull to the center of the earth. Through mathematics, he calculated that the moon is held in place by its proximity to us. I am indebted to Newton because he discovered that I am composed of particles that permit me to thrive through my own power. Family, blood, class are no obstacle to the right of the individual to grow. That is the new science: the new belief of modern man in himself to discover the truth by his own intelligence, in contradiction to the former belief in some sort of divine predestination or family.

EMILIE. Or gender.

VOLTAIRE. Or gender.

EMILIE. You profited by being banished to England.

VOLTAIRE. This is Newton's telescope. Look.

(He puts an arm around her shoulder and the telescope to her eye. She jumps in delight.)

EMILIE. Oh!

VOLTAIRE. Hold still. Concentrate. Breathe deeply. You can adjust it here.

EMILIE. I won't be able to live without a marvel such as this. May I have it?

VOLTAIRE. Better still, I'll teach you how to make one for yourself.

EMILIE. How can it be that this Englishman invents a telescope, was a mathematician, and investigated the cosmos?

VOLTAIRE. He is an example that one can be many things at once.

EMILIE. I must learn more of the master. Read.

VOLTAIRE. There is no translation of his work into French.

EMILIE. He wrote in English?

VOLTAIRE. In Latin. His *sistema mundi.*

EMILIE. His System of the World. How can I obtain his books?

VOLTAIRE. They are in my library. I smuggled them in.

EMILIE. The whole collection must be brought to my library in the country.

VOLTAIRE. They are sacred to me and must be within my sight.

EMILIE. Then you will just have to move in with me, Monsieur.

VOLTAIRE. Are you asking me to move in with you, Madame?

EMILIE. For as long as it takes to study the man's mind.

VOLTAIRE. His work is very difficult.

EMILIE. I am attracted by difficulty.

VOLTAIRE. And there are many volumes.

EMILIE. Do you have any objection to tutoring me on this new World System?

VOLTAIRE. On the contrary. I've been searching for ways to engender his teachings in French bosoms. But, I have one condition.

EMILIE. What condition?

VOLTAIRE. *(aside)* Women love to rebuild their homes. You say your country estate has not been improved since medieval times. I cannot submit my valuable books to the vagaries of the weather: storms, floods, leaky roofs, mildew, dampness. No. Fireplaces must be built, ceilings repaired, gutters installed. I envision a central common area, where we could meet after the working day. To enhance concentration and productivity, we should each have a separate wing constructed with working rooms. In the gardens canals must be dug to keep water from collecting near the foundations of the buildings, but could be redirected to irrigate –

EMILIE. Irrigate what?

VOLTAIRE. Vegetables are good for my digestion.

EMILIE. I would prefer to plant flowerbeds.

VOLTAIRE. I would pay for all the improvements, of course. But to save your husband from malicious gossip, we shall tell the world I have made him a construction loan. Do you think he might ambush us some night, kill us in our beds?

EMILIE. I've seen to it that the Minister of War has placed him in command of troops in Prussia. The advantage of marrying a military man is that they are rarely underfoot. And if he kills us, well…that's why we must work fast and hard. Death is always at our elbows. We must devote ourselves to the investigation of truth in secret and in silence, foreswear society. Live like monks!

VOLTAIRE. Yes! Live like monks! Devote ourselves only to scholarly pursuits! Abstinence and discipline!

EMILIE. Discipline and Abstinence! Foreswear society. Study! Research!

VOLTAIRE. Develop a body of work –

EMILIE. As you have done. Live on a higher plain!

VOLTAIRE. Seek only the truth!

EMILIE. Go naked in nature!

VOLTAIRE. Never again to wear a mask!

I can't squander a minute. Since I don't have long to live.

I have a plan of work to finish: My history of the reign of Louis XIV, dozens of tragedies, my view of Joan of Arc –

EMILIE. Oh, dear, you do play with fire. Don't you?

VOLTAIRE. I am playing with fire now, with you.

EMILIE. You are gambling.

VOLTAIRE. I believe that we meet the correct person for us maybe once in a life. I am not speaking of the numerous encounters we enjoy, but the chance of going beyond experimentation.

But my personal honor and love of truth compels me to warn you that if you become associated with me you will become known to the chief of police as the friend of a subversive man. The danger to your person is real. You assume that France is the zenith of civilization. No. Barely beneath the skin of our pride in oh-so-pretty achievements lies a barbaric disregard for the common man. Your inquisitive nature condemns you. Already you hide your intellectual labors in the countryside. But, your peace, I warn you, will be shattered by having my presence close by.

EMILIE. We will need a new library –

VOLTAIRE. Since we will be co-mingling our books –

EMILIE. A secret tunnel from your bedroom to mine–

VOLTAIRE. So that we can –

EMILIE. Read the Bible every night.

VOLTAIRE. We could start with Genesis.

EMILIE. What bliss.

VOLTAIRE. We must preserve our privacy.

EMILIE. From whom? The cows, the chickens…?

VOLTAIRE. The guests –

EMILIE. Guests?

VOLTAIRE. The greatest minds of our time. My friends.

EMILIE. I want your mind for myself alone.

VOLTAIRE. I need to learn the truth of the plays I plan to write in performance. I must construct a small theater where, after supper, we will enlist the aid of our guests to act.

EMILIE. A theater for you, and a laboratory for me. I am a legitimate scientist.

VOLTAIRE. You must prove it to me.

EMILIE. Do you think women were born only to deceive?

VOLTAIRE. Well, it is the only intellectual exercise allowed you.

EMILIE. Prejudice! I am similar to you. I have a man's mind in a woman's body. Alas.

VOLTAIRE. You are like myself, and I am like you, when we combine our particles we will become gods!

EMILIE. Oh, there is nothing more glorious than stimulating conversation.

VOLTAIRE. Over fine food, after a hard day's work. Not earlier than ten.

EMILIE. But what if I get hungry? I'm always hungry.

VOLTAIRE. Your appetite is a wonder. You've eaten half a shoulder of mutton, two thrushes and a dozen robins. From me, you will learn to fast and focus your mind. Discipline. You no longer have to gamble to make money, you have me. Are you cold? You're shaking.

EMILIE. If I am shaking, it is because the excitement I feel is immoderate. Cold? I am perspiring.

VOLTAIRE. Me, too. We've been talking through the night and my body aches.

(Sound of a trupmet)

VOLTAIRE. That's Maurice signaling we can continue.

EMILIE. To paradise!

(She spins. Her cloak bilows. Magically, we have arrived at het chateau in the country. Dogs bark. A welcoming bell rings.)

Welcome to my husband's chateau. Bienvenue.

VOLTAIRE. The walls are black. Was there a fire here? The servants are dressed in rags! Wore wooden clogs. Such misery.

EMILIE. We have no money.

When I was a child, I was spoiled by great luxury. My father was a trusted minister of the late king. My husband comes from a great family, but has no fortune. He earns but a small military salary. Now, I've learned to value those things that cannot be bought.

VOLTAIRE. How's that?

EMILIE. I am a serious scientist, look.

My laboratory! This is my weighing box.

VOLTAIRE. It's big and ugly, you shouldn't have it in your entrance hallway,

EMILIE. This is the only space large enough to contain all my scientific instruments.

VOLTAIRE. I will build you a proper laboratory.

EMILIE. This box is who I really am – big and ugly.

(He wanders over to the giant globe. Begins to caress it.)

Don't turn your back on me! I'm trying to explain to you the truth of my existence…

VOLTAIRE. Now this globe of the world is more like it…

EMILIE. Come away from there.

VOLTAIRE. I want to make love to you again and again right now on this globe. I love curves…

EMILIE. I want to describe to you an experiment

VOLTAIRE. Don't you want to be a great navigator sailing all over the globe with me?

EMILIE. No.

VOLTAIRE. Love is the stuff of nature embroidered by imagination.

EMILIE. Please, do not mention love.

Well-bred people never speak of it.

VOLTAIRE. But, you inspire –

EMILIE. Lust, perhaps. Love is not suited to my being. Pear trees can never bear pineapples.

People in my circle never speak of love.

VOLTAIRE. They don't?

EMILIE. Unless they are lying. Then it is acceptable.

VOLTAIRE. I am sincere. And insulted.

EMILIE. Do you know how many times you've used that word since we arrived? Three: "I love curves." "Can I make love to you again and again on that globe?" "Love is the stuff of nature…"

Cheap. Cheap. Cheap.

(He mops his brow with a handkerchief.)

VOLTAIRE. Do you have a dairy?

EMILIE. Would you like a glass of milk?

VOLTAIRE. Wouldn't you like a bath, after our long journey? I yearn to bathe in the milk of your cows. I wager your milk is the most delicious in France.

EMILIE. Science now.

VOLTAIRE. Scientifically speaking, the whole of your warm body is sensitive, but your lips especially are capable of a pleasure that is tireless.

EMILIE. I have been deceived. You are not a man, you are a mischievous monkey with a throbbing, red member tearing at your breeches. Well, take note, Monsieur Monkey, you are no longer in your wild bachelor domain, you are in…(mine)

…If you are to remain, as a privileged guest in my house, you must comply with your hostess's wishes: whatever she wants, whenever she wants – without question.

(He clutches his chest.)

VOLTAIRE. My heart…

(He collapses. She screams in alarm.)

…vinegar…vinegar…

EMILIE. I will send for the village physician to bleed you.

VOLTAIRE. No need. Madame, I am cursed with a nervous condition…that becomes aggravated when I become inflamed…my temperature shoots up…I am in a fever of lust…I must take to my bed. Won't you join me there?

EMILIE. Your insatiable desire is not flattering to me, In fact, I am insulted by it.

A horse for Monsieur Vulgár!

VOLTAIRE. Vulgár…!

(He starts moaning. Dogs start barking.)

EMILIE. Stop your moaning! Stop it! Love sick, are you? You are disturbing my household!

(calls) Quiet those dogs immediately!

VOLTAIRE. Mercy! Make me warm. Wrap me in your womanly limbs.

EMILIE. I humiliated myself going to your apartment in Paris because I couldn't wait to engage your sparkling imagination. Mercy?! You haven't a drop of it. Unlike you, I received no formal schooling. The only way I can learn is by listening for gold nuggets from the lips of wise men. THAT is my passion. There must be more to life. More. I WANT MORE!

VOLTAIRE. You are so demanding.

EMILIE. Stimulate my mind.

VOLTAIRE. *My* mind turns to vices.

EMILIE. No vices here.

VOLTAIRE. I must suffer censorship in the country, too!

EMILIE. Vices, then. But high-minded vices.

VOLTAIRE. Madame, no kingdom can flourish without vices. Take away the vanity of ladies of quality, and there will be no more making of fine silk.

(He attempts to place a hand on her bodice.)

EMILIE. Wear gloves when you touch me. Your hands are sweaty.

VOLTAIRE. I must touch you to know you're not merely a figment of my erotic imagination.

EMILIE. I am disappearing – I see it in your eyes. Prefer me not as an idealized woman in one of your plays. You are writing me now, aren't you? *Your* version of me. No wonder, Monsieur dramatist, you are doomed to dialogue by yourself. Men have trouble listening.

VOLTAIRE. I'm listening.

EMILIE. Look at me when you address me. Otherwise I feel you are excluding me.

VOLTAIRE. I'm sorry.

EMILIE. Was that the first time you apologized to anyone?

VOLTAIRE. Yes.

EMILIE. You made such a face.

VOLTAIRE. You are a very unhappy person.

EMILIE. I need to know that I can better myself. I need help. Be a mentor to me. Compassion is unknown in my world. I have only known cold, freezing cold. Warmth is considered a weakness. But *you* are not of my world. It is believed that the lower classes are hot. Dangerously so. And that the people of your world improve their station in life through education. You are a case in point. You attended the best Jesuit school in the land. And you left there armed with a head full of knowledge. I was not educated. I am a dumb, selfish aristocrat. Be generous with me. Help me find the path to perfection, please.

(beat)

VOLTAIRE. Was that the first time you said, "Please"?

EMILIE. Yes, my sweaty monkey.

I want you to esteem me. As I am. Or go. Frankly, I can pay more respectful men to teach me –

VOLTAIRE. No one in France can teach you the new science. The old science, which is to say Descartes, is based on theory, mental exercises. How much better to experience sweaty, hands-on proof – the way of the Englishman Newton teaches us a method of experimentation. Madam, you're a child – a beautiful one – but a totally ignorant one. I am besotted by you. And your brain – what a delight – if you really have one…

EMILIE. I really have one. I challenge you to discover it.

VOLTAIRE. Why has lasting love always eluded me? I'd like to discover that.

EMILIE. I'll have the globe moved to my bedroom.

VOLTAIRE. Thank you. And I'll bestow upon you my telescope.

EMILIE. Knowledge is so exciting!

VOLTAIRE. Now, describe your experiment.

EMILIE. I started a fire.

VOLTAIRE. Fire?

EMILIE. Under a piece of metal.

VOLTAIRE. It got very hot.

EMILIE. After the fire the metal weighed more.
The gases must have stuck to the metal. That's the extra weight I found. I measured the air. The oxygen lost weight. The exact amount that had increased the weight of the metal!

VOLTAIRE. And what is your conclusion?

EMILIE. That nothing disappears. There is a set amount of air, earth, water, and fire that will last through eternity. So, the energy you invest on the page will never be lost. You *are* immortal.

(beat)

VOLTAIRE. I love you.

(She covers his mouth.)

EMILIE. Hush.

VOLTAIRE. Thank you for affirming my existence.

(Beat. Sounds of approaching horseman.)

Listen. Soldiers are coming to arrest us! Kill us! Put out my eyes!

(He hands her a card.)

Quickly. Take this. He is a friend in London. Maurice will make certain you find safe passage.

(He hands her a small bag.)

Here. Hide this bag of gold between your breasts. Go. Rouse the peasants. I will keep the soldiers busy while you make your escape. I will never forget our picnic in the snow.

EMILIE. Nor I.

(commotion outside)

Are you prepared to die for me?

VOLTAIRE. I am.

EMILIE. Is this what it's like to live with a wanted man?

VOLTAIRE. Yes.

EMILIE. *I* want you!

VOLTAIRE. So do the bloodthirsty forces of repression. Who want to torture me.

(He kisses her passionately.)

Now go.

Save yourself.

(With a spank he sends her off. He speaks to the audience:)

I find the woman of my dreams, now I must lose her. *(She runs back in.)*

EMILIE. THE METEOR SHOWER!

VOLTAIRE. So, we'll die looking at the stars!

(The curtain falls.)

ACT TWO

(Begins ten years later and spans from 1743 to 1749. Chateau de Cirey - the country estate of Emilie du Chatelet.)

*(**VOLTAIRE** is writing lying on **EMILIE**'s sumptuous bed. As usual he works on his portable desk equipped with ink pot, blotting powder and beautiful feather pens. At hand is coffee, writing paper and candles. He wears a flowing red robe.)*

VOLTAIRE. How to sustain it?

I am in love. But is lasting love possible without humiliation? I want to make Emilie happy, so she won't go running back to Paris.

(He goes back to writing.)

She, in the freshness of her youth – oh, what could he say about such an eager pupil? She absorbed everything he taught her.

He wanted to relive her questions – about science, about life –

(writes) They agreed to meet – not during the day when each of them attended to their personal labors – but to wait until ten every night when they had supper. They pondered the great mysteries of life, and sleep solved all the problems of mankind.

They found magic in those first ten years, which passed like the wind. She grew in bravery. Became more like him. Took her life into her hands everyday. They did not waste one moment – whether for pleasure or to produce new pages of scientific data or poetic truth. They lived very much as if they had no future.

Their perilous euphoria made them criminals in the eyes of the state.

EMILIE. *(her head pops out from beneath the covers)* Would you please go write in your bath and leave my bed!

(She jumps out of bed and goes behind a curtian)

VOLTAIRE. I need the warm scent of your bedclothes to inspire the masterwork I'm writing about you.

EMILIE. *(off)* Come help me dress. Earn your keep.

VOLTAIRE. What happened to the bag of gold I gave you on that magical night of the meteor shower.

EMILIE. *(off)* That was 10 years ago.

VOLTAIRE. That gold was to save your life.

EMILIE. *(off)* It did. That night I played cards with the soldiers, I made sure I lost. That bag of gold has bought us ten years free from the Queens guards. There is an advantage to making friends with the regiment. I am a student of male energy.

VOLTAIRE. Common people are the energy that fuels this feudal estate. They are the soul of mankind.
As a favor to me, will you please go visit the peasants in their homes.

EMILIE. *(off)* Why?

VOLTAIRE. You wish to master the physical world, these people and their children are an important part of it.

EMILIE. *(off)* Important?!

*(**EMILIE** appears dressed as a man. He is shocked.)*

VOLTAIRE. Am I now supposed to put on a dress?

EMILIE. Must you always be the opposite of me?

VOLTAIRE. We are not the same.

EMILIE. Adam sacrificed a rib to create a companion, to heal his loneliness.

VOLTAIRE. We really must look into Genesis.

EMILIE. When I return.

VOLTAIRE. From?

EMILIE. Paris.

(beat)

I am to present a report of an experiment at the Café Gardot.

VOLTAIRE. Yes, scientists gather there.

EMILIE. Since women are not permitted in coffee shops…

VOLTAIRE. You will fool no one.

EMILIE. I will pretend to be you.

VOLTAIRE. Then represent me well.

(She starts to leave.)

Don't go. There have been uprisings in the villages.

EMILIE.; I am to be escorted by my soldier friends from the garrison.

VOLTAIRE. Farewell.

EMILIE. Farewell.

(She goes. Sound of horse galloping off.)

VOLTAIRE. He'd lost her. He'd lost her for sure. A soul for which mine was made. She has chosen to be escorted to Paris by her soldier friends. Paris her artistocratic friends call to her. As do men in uniform from noble families. He gave her is heart, his essence – Totally. He was spent.

(clutches his heart)

He felt painful fingernails clawing at my heart. Oh, the pain of her departure! I die! I die! To think he would die without ever having heard her sweet voice say to him, "I love you." Weeks passed.

(She returns. Her head is wrapped in a bloody bandage.)

VOLTAIRE. What happened?

EMILIE. Nothing. I am not made of sugar.

(He begins to unwrap her wound, cure her.)

VOLTAIRE. I did a tremendous amount of work in your absence.

EMILIE. I will catch up to you.

VOLTAIRE. Why did you come back?

EMILIE. To protect you.

VOLTAIRE. What happened?

EMILIE. I made a stupid mistake. I stopped at a village for a cup of soup. The cook overcharged me. I refused to pay and a crowd of women and children turned on me.

VOLTAIRE. You're so cheap.

EMILIE. But I'm a good swordsman. I brought this pamphlet from Paris. Our enemies are trying to discredit our ideas.

(She holds a pamphlet. Turns aside.)

(aside) I am now coupled publicly with my low-born lover by the anti-intellectual crowd.

They are circulating this libelous pamphlet that shows...

(looks at pamphlet)

...us in an...an erotic illustration.

VOLTAIRE. Oh My!

EMILIE. Mercy! Conservatives are so dirty-minded. We are not named, of course, but – I am bending backward over a globe of the world. Books scattered about. There must be a spy in the house.

The explanation under the cartoon reads that two intellectuals are practicing adulterous free love. And contends that depravity of the body leads to depravity of the mind.

*(She hands the pamphlet to **VOLTAIRE**.)*

EMILIE. Luckily my dress is covering my face.

VOLTAIRE. But you are the only woman educated enough to own a globe.

EMILIE. Education has ruined my reputation.

VOLTAIRE. I cannot permit you to be sullied in public. I will return to Paris and thrash those cowards!

EMILIE. No!

VOLTAIRE. Even if I am arrested –

EMILIE. No!

VOLTAIRE. Even if I am put in chains!

EMILIE. No.

VOLTAIRE. I don't care if I am burned at the stake.

EMILIE. *(aside)* Oh, he loves the tussle of Paris.

VOLTAIRE. *(calls)* Saddle my horse!

EMILIE. No.

VOLTAIRE. Polish my sword!

EMILIE. No, no, no. You are to do nothing.

VOLTAIRE. I do not turn the other cheek.

(She grabs his head, kisses his cheek.)

EMILIE. I cannot live without your kisses.

(He begins to melt.)

Turn your passion toward me.

VOLTAIRE. I am a man of action!

EMILIE. You are a man of words.

Besides, I rather like being described as an intellectual. A mental companion of yours. Actually, it was an honor. Maybe the greatest public recognition I've ever received.

VOLTAIRE. *(writing)* To please her, he used his knowledge of British gardens to create romantic waterfalls, fountains. He built an enchanted lake for her – to mirror the full moon and the galaxies. After dinner she liked it when he lay her on a floating bed and pushed her across the water, as she sang –

There have been times when I've felt I was disappearing, that she was annihilating him. I am supreme in matter of creativity, but oh, she has such a mastery of numbers! And her brilliant brain works so rapidly, her fingers could not command the words and numbers to fill pages with lucidity. So, when they write together, she dictated her finding to him. And he followed dutifully behind her thoughtful lead. Was she unmanning him?

EMILIE. I think I am surpassing your production of 100 letters a day. The University of Bologna is considering me a candidate for its prestigious Academy of Sciences. Aren't you proud of me.

VOLTAIRE. So…You have been rewarded…I applaud you.

(He does, slowly, rather half-heartedly.)

You should have warned me that so many handsome Italian messengers were coming.

(She picks up a book.)

EMILIE. Read to me in bed.

VOLTAIRE. No, I have to do work of my own.

EMILIE. Well then, I'm off to feed my poor people.

(picks up basket)

You must supervise the workmen. I detest concerning myself with household improvements. I leave that in your hands.

(sounds of hammering)

VOLTAIRE. You say you destest concerning yourself with household improvements. But you can't resist changing staircases into chimneys and chimneys into staircases.

(to workmen)

Gentlemen, that will be the site of the new theater.

EMILIE. *(voice)* No. It is a perfect place for a salon.

VOLTAIRE. Emilie…! You left the construction in my hands.

EMILIE. *(voice)* Those are my orders.

VOLTAIRE. The theater I'm making will be better than the little theater at Versailles. The only reason some of my plays fail in Paris is because the stage of the Comedie is totally antiquated.

EMILIE. The reason some of your plays fail is because they are bad!

(She goes off singing merely.)

(He sneezes, pulls out a huge handkerchief.)

(She tosses him a red nightcap.)

VOLTAIRE. What's this ugly thing?

EMILIE. Wear it and you'll stop sneezing. To think I have to take care of armies of peasants and the old philosopher, too!

VOLTAIRE. I thought you liked sick men?

EMILIE. Not with me under the covers.

(She goes off singing. He puts on the cap and looks in a hand mirror. Touches his nose.)

VOLTAIRE. I look like a court fool. Well, that's what he was – a clown. Offered sanctuary from the police in country homes, I always endeavored to amuse my hosts. Was he doomed forever to be an outcast? A house guest.

(She returns with an empty basket.)

EMILIE. Are you going to look in my mirror all day while I go to labor in the fields. Go back to your own room.

(She takes the mirror and studies herself.)

Men are so vain. I have a new policy: I don't give out food unless the people first listen to me sing. Bread and a song. Isn't that nice? I feed their bellies and their craving for culture.

VOLTAIRE. What else is wrong with my plays?

EMILIE. Will you be stewing about that all day?

I beg you not to give orders to the workers in your bathrobe. It's so low class.

(He re-arranges his robe.)

VOLTAIRE. There! Now I look like a Roman senator.

EMILIE. Scientists are seeking me out and we haven't enough bedrooms to house them yet. Bedrooms, build more bedrooms.

VOLTAIRE. *(to workmen)* You, gardeners! Here we shall plant elms.

EMILIE. Limes!

VOLTAIRE. *(to workmen)* Drain the marshes. Plant herbs here, and vegetables over there. Vegetables are good for my digestion.

EMILIE. Flowers, flowers. Annuals –

VOLTAIRE. Perennials.

(They sit to play cards.)

VOLTAIRE. I disapprove of you sneaking out with mountains of food. You're not only feeding the poor, you're feeding yourself. And you're starting to look plump. That tells me that I do not fill you.

EMILIE. You don't.

VOLTAIRE. Abstinence, discipline.

EMILIE. It's true that I'm famished. But that is my nature.

VOLTAIRE. You're famished and yet you were late for supper last night.

EMILIE. That was no reason to break down the door of my study.

VOLTAIRE. You were closeted up there for hours with that Italian mathematician.

EMILIE. I needed verification of my equations.

VOLTAIRE. And he can't even act.

EMILIE. That was no reason to send him away.

VOLTAIRE. He's been here three months. There's altogether too much science going on around here!

EMILIE. On the contrary, there is altogether too much theater around here!

VOLTAIRE. He who condemns the theater is an enemy to his country!

EMILIE. If you employ all our guests on the stage, we're not going to have an audience.

VOLTAIRE. I'm having an artist paint figures to occupy the seats. Soon you will play to the Empress of Russia, the Pope, Joan of Arc…

EMILIE. You continue to dip your pen in acid. No more coffee for you.

VOLTAIRE. Why?

EMILIE. Coffee makes men impotent.

VOLTAIRE. Man can only have a number of teeth, hair and sexual ideas. There comes a time when he necessarily loses his teeth, his hair and…

EMILIE. The wittiest man in Europe is not funny at home. Why have you turned cold to me? Not one love note. I search in the pages of my books for a poem. No. I go mad looking in the hollows of trees for some sweet present or surprising words penned by your hand…

VOLTAIRE. If I've turned cold it's because you've become an engineer! Smudges on your face, stains on your dresses…

EMILIE. And you've become a…a wife!

VOLTAIRE. Better a wife than one of those strutting, stupid cavalry boys stationed at the garrison.

EMILIE. They carry my packages on market days.

VOLTAIRE. You shop too much.

EMILIE. I support the porcelain industry.

VOLTAIRE. All your life, your deepest heart is drawn to fighting men.

EMILIE. Is there any more handsome sight than boys from noble families in uniform, sitting astride their high-stepping steeds on parade. Gallant! Drums…banners…

VOLTAIRE. I am a pacifist.

EMILIE. You are not patriotic.

VOLTAIRE. I don't approve of you riding all over our lands with them.

EMILIE. You ride me so infrequently in your old age.

VOLTAIRE. I understand that you are so much younger than I and require playmates to gallop about with.

EMILIE. A safety measure. To protect me when I collect the rents.

VOLTAIRE. It's one thing to collect the rents and another to allow those noisy boys to swim in our lake. Without their uniforms. It's a scandal…!

EMILIE. "Our" lake, "our" lands!?

VOLTAIRE. Well, I am the master here, in your husband's absence.

EMILIE. So now I have a husband and a wife!

VOLTAIRE. You're a handful. Hand over the rents.

EMILIE. What?!

VOLTAIRE. From now on I will administrate the rents paid by our tenant farmers.

EMILIE. What arrogance! You think you own me AND my lands! Just because you make a few little improvements here and there…

VOLTAIRE. Four hundred thousand worth.

EMILIE. Are you saying you've purchased the right to my company?

VOLTAIRE. You ARE a bit of a whore.

EMILIE. What a trap you have laid for me – encouraging my extravagances, leading me to believe in freedom! Equality! You are not enlightened. You are a fraud. No, your writings will not outlive you because you have the heart of a merchant.

VOLTAIRE. Your husband warned me that you are not to be trusted with money.

EMILIE. When?

VOLTAIRE. He arranged a visit with me while you were in town, distracting some of the young soldiers.

EMILIE. He visits *you* and not *me*?

VOLTAIRE. He was angry that you don't send him shipments of limes – So that's why you wanted avenues of lime trees. To please HIM!

EMILIE. What else?

VOLTAIRE. He's heard you've started gambling again at neighboring estates.

EMILIE. If I gamble, it is on your behalf. After all, if you want the local nobility to perform in your new plays, there must be a bit of recompense for all their hard work. I like to work hard and play hard but it is a hardship for our guests.

VOLTAIRE. Actors in Paris love me. I share my earnings with them.

EMILIE. I don't think we're going to have many visitors anymore, since the unrest in the country side has spread. And we are caught in the middle – the King hates you and the lower classes beyond our gates hate me.

I read letter after letter about intellectuals who have disappeared from the streets, taken by the secret police, tortured, their bodies found floating in the Seine. Spies everywhere, informers.

There is a fear that a rural uprising could start here. Our neighbors report that we foster a better life for the laborers by teaching them to read and other skills above their station.

I haven't been able to sleep.

I feel faint.

VOLTAIRE. Do you want me to put you to bed?

EMILIE. Oh, would you?

(With great tenderness, he helps her to undress.)

VOLTAIRE. Don't worry about our laborers. I have let it be known that I've been corresponding with the Pope. And that his Holiness has suggested I dramatize religious events—to make the story of the birth of Christ more immediate to the common people. They must be a part of our family.

You must teach the people to sing the seasonal hymns.

EMILIE. I hoped to hide from you the avalanche of troubles out there in the dark.

VOLTAIRE. May I bathe you, soothe you?

(He gets a bowl and a sponge and gives her a sponge bath during the following. She doesn't resist.)

EMILIE. Work on the encyclopedia has stopped.

VOLTAIRE. We are going into a dark, mindless period, indeed.

EMILIE. There is much fear at Versailles. When the king appears, he is not cheered. We sacrifice thousands of

EMILIE. *(cont.)* lives on foreign battlefields, the poor are taxed to pay for the carnage, and when anyone questions, they are called unpatriotic. No one is safe.

(He puts his arms around her.)

VOLTAIRE. Be strong. What we have accomplished here over the years is undeniable. For whatever time we have left, we must continue to work, as an example to others. Knowledge is a kiss from God.

EMILIE. I want to translate Newton for my son Louis. The latest book on physics still in use is 80 years old. He is proving to have a talent for abstract thinking. His calculations in the field combine mathematics and vision. He can aim a cannon and predict precisely where the cannonball will fall.

VOLTAIRE. He is using the calculus his mother learned from Newton.

EMILIE. The calculus you taught me. The boy is a wonder.

VOLTAIRE. You have an ability to synthesize an abstract thought with remarkable clarity.

EMILIE. Compose a bedtime tale for me.

VOLTAIRE. Very well. But I need the moonlight to inspire me. Permit me to transport you over the water of our enchanted lake. There is a full moon.

EMILIE. Always a dangerous time.

(He picks up a tall pole, stands on the bed and pushes down, sending the bed-boat out onto the lake. A moon appears. She makes herself comfortable on her many pillows, lets a hand dip into the water. There is a soft breeze and the sounds of cicadas mating in the trees. They travel a bit in silence.)

The cicadas are mating in the trees. Listen.

VOLTAIRE. Listen to my story.

EMILIE. I listen.

VOLTAIRE. Once upon a time, an old gallant fell in love with the most learned lady in the land. She was younger than he and he could no longer satisfy her. His body could not produce fire.

(She pats the cushions beside her. He lifts the pole onto the boat and climbs on the bed beside her.)

VOLTAIRE. *(cont.)* Once upon a time he was volcanic, his body would tremble with a frightening roar of coming desire so terrible that all the barnyard animals would run away to hide in expectation of a giant cataclysm. It was reported that the roaring master of the house so ached for fulfillment that the peasants saw electrical sparks in the night air. She saw stars shooting across the night sky, the cicadas played their music, the earth was alive in anticipation of sexual harmony. Do you remember?

EMILIE. Yes.

VOLTAIRE. I can no longer accomplish such feats of nature, my dear. Perhaps, I was a living flame for too long, too often. I was never a healthy man. I am burned away.

EMILIE. What were you called, as a little boy? Tell me, I love secrets.

VOLTAIRE. Zozo. Say it.

EMILIE. Zozo.

VOLTAIRE. The last woman to call me that was my mother.

EMILIE. Look, the dawn. We've talked through the night yet again.

(He docks the bed-boat. He helps her to get on land.)

How sad. Soon it will be too cold to go out on the lake.

VOLTAIRE. But we will be able to do some ice dancing when the lake freezes.

EMILIE. We have been here almost sixteen years.

(A bell rings.)

VOLTAIRE. The bell calling the peasants to the fields.

EMILIE. Help me to dress.

VOLTAIRE. I *have* become your servant, and I don't mind at all.

EMILIE. My chambermaid.

(He dresses her.)

Zozo, come here.

VOLTAIRE. We had a monkey called Zozo. He was always getting into mischief.

EMILIE. Children suffer.

VOLTAIRE. Not the children who live here.

EMILIE. The peasants eat white bread now.

VOLTAIRE. It's a scandal.

EMILIE. It's an experiment.

VOLTAIRE. An act of faith.

EMILIE. An act of love.

VOLTAIRE. Did I hear you correctly?

EMILIE. Yes.

VOLTAIRE. Say it once more.

EMILIE. I find that I love you.

VOLTAIRE. THE MARQUISE DU CHATELET FINDS THAT PEAR TREES CAN BEAR PINEAPPLES!

EMILIE. And do you know when I knew?

VOLTAIRE. When?

EMILIE. When I was teaching the common people to sing for Christmas. It was during the "Gloria." My voice was never more effortless. From the tips of my toes up through my body.

VOLTAIRE. Thank you for letting me count your teeth on so many cold evenings. I love your mouth on summer evenings as well.

EMILIE. Thank you for telling me important things. You're the only man who has.

VOLTAIRE. Here, take my gold clock…

(takes out his pocket clock, removes it from its chain, hands it to her)

…as a token of…

EMILIE. This timepiece is holy to you.

VOLTAIRE. *You* are holy to me, proof that there is a merciful God. But, I always carried it as another more scientific verification of His existence. If the world runs as perfectly as a clock, there has to be a clockmaker.

(She opens that watch.)

EMILIE. Where is my portrait? Who is this young woman?

VOLTAIRE. My poor niece. She's become a widow,

EMILIE. She's lovely. *(opens mail)* Listen –

Cardinal Fleury has died. His chair has now become vacant in the Academy. If I can help to give you what you want, I'll move heaven and earth.

VOLTAIRE. But, if I'm rejected once again?

EMILIE. Will you forgive me everything, if I fight for your election to the Academy?

VOLTAIRE. What have you done that's so terrible?

EMILIE. Do you agree?

VOLTAIRE. I agree.

EMILIE. It will be difficult for you to fill the seat vacated by a Cardinal. I am central to your problem. We are living in sin. But we aren't committing adultery anymore, are we? I will let it be known that I've become a penitent, that I've banished you from my bed…I will give up putting rouge on my breasts, I will sell my diamonds and build a chapel right here where we stand.

(beat)

What is it?

VOLTAIRE. I can't speak.

EMILIE. For the first time in your miserable life.

(He kisses her hand lovingly.)

One of my young military friends has made me pregnant.

VOLTAIRE. You have despised me for years, attempted to diminish me, humiliate me, destroy me. You are a selfish woman.

EMILIE. Selfish!? You denied me your body for so long, selfish. For sixteen years your aristocratic schoolmates and I have conspired to keep you out of prison; lying to the Chief of Police that your treasonous sentiments were written by others, that you were contrite about what you said, selfish!? I have lost face, prestige, living with you. I've had to overcome the scorn of my family and friends, who considered that my choice of you was many steps down the ladder. So far down, that I was viewed as being an unnatural person for consorting with another species.

VOLTAIRE. Well, now you have consorted with a man of your species so everyone in Paris will be very happy.

EMILIE. Maybe that is why we could not make a child – because I was a woman and you were a monkey.

VOLTAIRE. I gave you everything. But, I was unable to substitute your common sexual hunger with intellectual satisfaction. Oh, how I awaited your maturity, waited for you to take your place here beside me as a great, noble, selfless person. But, no, you remain an aristocrat. I created myself. But I could not reproduce myself. I will not live. While you and yours, who are worthless will live on and on

EMILIE. Why is it that other men – famous mathematicians, counselors to the king – think me serious

VOLTAIRE. Ha, they do not live with you. They do not know that your attention span –

EMILIE. That is unfair!

VOLTAIRE. You can't sustain, my dear. Women by nature create in short spurts. Little orgasmic pops. While men through time are noted for epic longevity. We are big.

EMILIE. You are neither big, nor fertile.

VOLTAIRE. I have an immense body of work

EMILIE. If the world only knew how much of that body was given birth by me.

VOLTAIRE. Cheap, cheap, cheap. It is impossible to have a big fight with you. Well, you have condemned yourself to obscurity. To life in the country with your brat.

EMILIE. I wish you were the father.

VOLTAIRE. I wish I were, too.

(beat)

Why did I want to punish you? I withheld the affirmation of my body just as your scientific fame began to bear fruit.

I wanted you to exercise restraint; discipline of the mind and the body. But, instead, I encouraged your sexual sport.

(laughs)

I…I AM the father.

(laughs)

I am a fool. An immortal court jester. A failure.

EMILIE. You are free to return to Paris. Pompadour has convinced the King that only you can write a dramatic ballet that will be the centerpiece of his birthday festivities.

VOLTAIRE. And she secured apartments for me at Versailles. Yes. I've known that I could return for some time.

EMILIE. You must leave at once.

VOLTAIRE. The birth that will take place here is far more important, I'll stay.

EMILIE. You have become a very noble man, indeed.

VOLTAIRE. No, I am a merchant. Horse breeding, bee keeping, cloth for military uniforms. Please write to your husband and tell him that if he can secure a military contract, there will be a sizeable profit for him.

EMILIE. Tell him yourself. I've written him to come.

VOLTAIRE. Oh, you are going to sleep with him so that when the time comes he and the world will believe the child is his.

(She slaps him.)

EMILIE. When the time comes, I will not survive it. I've seen healthy, younger women die from child-bed fever. I am forty-three years old. We make great mental leaps you and I, but medicine is in a sorry state. I want to work. Use the time remaining to complete my translation of Newton.

VOLTAIRE. I will transfer all my candles to your office.

(He bows in leave-taking.)

Madame…

EMILIE. Thank you. How many candles do you think I'll need? A night?

VOLTAIRE. Twenty. The baby will be born at your desk.

EMILIE. I never thought I would be able to keep you from the intellectual life of Paris for so long.

VOLTAIRE. To be barred from my beloved city only enhanced my reputation among my followers. I have become more celebrated by being here, a victim of censorship and monarchical tyranny.

Work is our salvation, you and I.

EMILIE. I wrote to my husband to come – you see this is the sort of thing a man of your class couldn't understand. I wrote him to come because it is the proper thing to do when one does not expect to live. I am still the mother of his son. And there are matters of property. We have amassed a library of more than 20,000 volumes. My husband has never read a book in his life. I need you to help me finish my great work on modern physics.

It is important to present the world of ideas in its global context.

We must introduce Newton AND extend him. Metaphysics must be brought into the picture to prove the sufficient reason for the universe. From the most physical of science to the existence of God.

VOLTAIRE. You have never looked more beautiful to my eyes.

EMILIE. I am in a state of grace.

VOLTAIRE. When we are confronted by the great moments in life, we turn to the kingdom of God.

EMILIE. As you've said, if God didn't exist we'd have to invent Him.

VOLTAIRE. Secretly, I've watched you teaching the farmers to sing with such fervor.

I have never told you that my father was an accountant. One morning, he took me with him to your apartments overlooking the fragrant orange trees. When we were climbing the marble staircase, my father told me the place had 30 rooms and that you had 17 servants. I heard you laughing, looked down at an interior courtyard, and there you were, receiving a fencing lesson. You had the most beautiful legs I'd ever seen. You have disturbed my vision of the world ever since.

EMILIE. Work with me.

(beat)

And after you are dead, you will be known for having worked with *me.*

(to audience)

I get up at nine now, sometimes at eight, I work till three; then I take coffee; I resume work at four. At ten I stop to eat a morsel; I talk to Monsieur Voltaire; at midnight I go to work again, and keep on till five in the morning. I find Monsieur Voltaire fast asleep in an armchair outside my door, the pages of my manuscript on his lap and scattered all over the floor.

I was cursed with curiosity. I sought knowledge, I did not seek love. But, curiously, I found it. Monseiur Voltaire said that knowledge is a kiss from God. Monseiur Voltaire kissed me. And bestowed upon me his divine knowledge. With a smile.

(Through the following, she stands proudly, radiantly.
VOLTAIRE *senses her presence.)*

VOLTAIRE. I received word today that I was elected to the Academy of Arts.

EMILIE. You are immortal.

VOLTAIRE. The greatest problem known to man – how do we keep the people we love alive? How do we stop reducing our life companion to nothingness? Emilie gave birth to a little daughter. Both died of child-bed fever. I almost did not survive this loss. But, made sure that her writings found their way into print. Emilie's books are in my library. Her remarkable translation of the work of Sir Isaac Newton is read by young men in all the schools in France. And will be for centuries to come. Her son Louis died at the guillotine. While I was lifted onto the shoulders of cheering revolutionaries. Oh, and now in the latter part of my life, I started a love affair with my niece. Apparently, I wasn't impotent after all.

(addresses the Members of the Academy)

Gentlemen of the Academy: I know it is customary for a new member to speak of the man he is replacing in glowing terms. But, today, before this august body, I wish to break the rules, and speak instead of a woman, who, by all rights, should have been honored by you in her lifetime.

It was New Year's Eve in Paris, the night she changed his miserable life. Our stupid, though handsome, hero was invited to see the royal fireworks from the terrace of a treacherous aristocrat. He was standing behind a beautiful woman seated at a gaming table.

*(**EMILIE** appears wearing her golden half mask and holding a tall candle)*

(curtain)

ABOUT THE AUTHOR

ARTHUR GIRON's latest play is *St. Francis in Egypt,* and he is co-writing the book for a musical *Amazing Grace.* He was named "one of the best contemporary dramatists" by critic Rosette LaMont. His plays are performed continuously throughout the country. *Becoming Memories* (published by Samuel French) won a Los Angeles Critics Drama-Logue Award for "Outstanding Achievement in Writing." It has been seen in over 70 cities. *The New York Times* described his play Edith Stein (also published by Samuel French) as being "filled with passionate ideas." It will be seen in Buenos Aires. His play *Flight* (published by Samuel French) toured 120 cities. He is a founding member of the Ensemble Studio Theatre, which produced his plays *Moving Bodies* (published by Samuel French), *Innocent Pleasures,* and *Boys Dies Dancing Mambo* (Money). Other plays include *The Coffee Trees, A Dream of Wealth, Charley Bacon and His Family, Scouts Honor* (Dirty Jokes) and *Emilie's Voltaire,* which was awarded the Galileo Prize.

Also by
Arthur Giron...

Becoming Memories

Edith Stein

Flight

Moving Bodies